This diary belongs to

Kitty

BABY-SITTERS
Little Sister

Secret Diary

Ann M. Martin

A
LITTLE APPLE
PAPERBACK

SCHOLASTIC INC.
New York Toronto London Auckland Sydney

Cover art by Susan Tang

Interior art by Shannon M. McIntyre

ISBN 0-590-45010-7

12 11 10 9 8 7 6 5 4 3   1 2 3 4 5 6/9

Printed in the U.S.A.   40

First Scholastic printing, May 1991

A NOTE FROM KAREN

HI! I'M KAREN BREWER.
I'M SEVEN YEARS OLD.
I LIKE TO DO LOTS OF THINGS.
I LIKE TO ROLLER-SKATE.
I LIKE TO EAT ICE CREAM.
AND I ESPECIALLY LIKE TO
KEEP SECRETS.
THIS DIARY IS PERFECT FOR
KEEPING SECRETS.
YOU CAN WRITE DOWN YOUR
MOST SPECIAL THOUGHTS
AND FEELINGS.
AND YOU CAN ANSWER
QUESTIONS ALL ABOUT YOU!

LOVE,
Karen Brewer

7 years old!

blue

eye

brown

Sue TALL

TOM

Karen

8 years old.

Short

All About Me!

My name is _Kitty_.

I am _8_ years old.

The color of my hair is _Brown_.

I am _____ feet _____ inches tall.

My address is

_____

_____

_____.

My phone number is _391-6689_.

Today's Date Is: _____

Things I Did Today: _____

_____

_____

_____

_____

_____

_____

_____

_____

_____

_____

_____

_____

_____

_____

_____

Today's Date Is: _____

Things I Did Today: _____

_____
_____
_____
_____
_____
_____
_____
_____
_____
_____
_____
_____
_____
_____
_____

Today's Date Is: _____

Things I Did Today: _____

_____

_____

_____

_____

_____

_____

_____

_____

_____

_____

_____

_____

_____

_____

_____

_____

_____

_____

Today's Date Is: _____

Things I Did Today: _____

_____

_____

_____

_____

_____

_____

_____

_____

_____

_____

_____

_____

_____

_____

_____

Today's Date Is: _____

Things I Did Today: _____

_____
_____
_____
_____
_____
_____
_____
_____
_____
_____
_____
_____
_____
_____
_____

Today's Date Is: _____

Things I Did Today: _____

_____

_____

_____

_____

_____

_____

_____

_____

_____

_____

_____

_____

_____

_____

Today's Date Is: _____

Things I Did Today: _____

_____

_____

_____

_____

_____

_____

_____

_____

_____

_____

_____

_____

_____

_____

_____

_____

Today's Date Is: _____

Things I Did Today: _____

_____

_____

_____

_____

_____

_____

_____

_____

_____

_____

_____

_____

_____

_____

Today's Date Is: _____

Things I Did Today: _____

_____

_____

_____

_____

_____

_____

_____

_____

_____

_____

_____

_____

_____

_____

_____

_____

Today's Date Is: _____

Things I Did Today: _____

_____

_____

_____

_____

_____

_____

_____

_____

_____

_____

_____

_____

_____

_____

_____

_____

Today's Date Is: _____

Things I Did Today: _____

_____
_____
_____
_____
_____
_____
_____
_____
_____
_____
_____
_____
_____
_____
_____
_____
_____

Today's Date Is: _____

Things I Did Today: _____

_____
_____
_____
_____
_____
_____
_____
_____
_____
_____
_____
_____
_____
_____

Today's Date Is: _____

Things I Did Today: _____

_____

_____

_____

_____

_____

_____

_____

_____

_____

_____

_____

_____

_____

_____

_____

_____

Today's Date Is: _____

Things I Did Today: _____

_____

_____

_____

_____

_____

_____

_____

_____

_____

_____

_____

_____

_____

_____

_____

_____

Today's Date Is: _____

Things I Did Today: _____

_____

_____

_____

_____

_____

_____

_____

_____

_____

_____

_____

_____

_____

_____

_____

_____

Today's Date Is: _____

Things I Did Today: _____

_____

_____

_____

_____

_____

_____

_____

_____

_____

_____

_____

_____

_____

_____

Today's Date Is: _____

Things I Did Today: _____

_____
_____
_____
_____
_____
_____
_____
_____
_____
_____
_____
_____
_____
_____
_____
_____

Today's Date Is: _____

Things I Did Today: _____

_____
_____
_____
_____
_____
_____
_____
_____
_____
_____
_____
_____
_____
_____

Today's Date Is: _____

Things I Did Today: _____

_____

_____

_____

_____

_____

_____

_____

_____

_____

_____

_____

_____

_____

_____

_____

Today's Date Is: _____

Things I Did Today: _____

_____

_____

_____

_____

_____

_____

_____

_____

_____

_____

_____

_____

_____

_____

_____

_____

Friends R Fun

Karen's best friends are Hannie Papadakis and Nancy Dawes. Who are your best friends?

Name _____

Address _____

_____

Phone Number _____

Name _____

Address _____

_____

Phone Number _____

Name _____

Address _____

_____

Phone Number _____

Nancy **Friends 4 ever!** Hannie

mom SAM Andrew Dad
Kristy ELIZABETH Nannie
Charlie David Michael
Emily Michelle Seth

Family Facts

Karen has lots of people in her family. She has a mother, a father, and a stepfamily, too!

How many people are in your family? (Don't forget to count yourself!) _____ 4 _____

How many brothers do you have? _____ 0 _____
Names _____ — _____
Ages _____ — _____

How many sisters? _____ 1 _____
Names _____ angela _____
Ages _____ 11 _____

Do you have any stepbrothers or stepsisters?
_____ no _____

Pets

Emily Junior is Karen's pet rat. Karen named her after her adopted sister, Emily Michelle.

Do you have any pets?

dog ___no___

cat ___no___

fish ___no___

bird ___no___

other ___no___

What are your pets' names? ___I don't have a pet___

What kinds of pets do your friends have? ___a hamster___

If you could have any pet in the world, what would it be? ___a dog___

Sports I Like

Karen loves to roller-skate with her friends.

What sports do you like?

softball _____ no _____

basketball _____ yes _____

gymnastics _____ yes _____

ballet _____ no _____

jumping rope _____ yes _____

ice-skating _____ yes _____

soccer _____ yes _____

swimming _____ yes _____

other _____ & roller skating _____

JUMP ROPE

Fun Things I Like to Do

Karen likes to play hopscotch with a special stone she keeps in her desk at school.

What are some fun things you like to do?

play dress up _____ no _____

jump rope _____ yes _____

ride my bike _____ yes _____

play hopscotch _____ yes _____

sing songs _____ no _____

other _____

Book Nook

Once, Karen got to meet one of her favorite authors at the local bookstore.

What are some of your favorite books?

1. _All of the litter sitter book_
2. _Robert much books_
3. _____
4. _____

THE POLAR EXPRESS

Paddington

Doctor Dolittle

Bobbsey Twins

Who is your favorite author?

Ann M martin

If you could meet your favorite author, what would you say to him or her? _that am M Martin is the best_

Today's Date Is: _____

Things I Did Today: _____

_____

_____

_____

_____

_____

_____

_____

_____

_____

_____

_____

_____

_____

_____

Today's Date Is: _____

Things I Did Today: _____

_____

_____

_____

_____

_____

_____

_____

_____

_____

_____

_____

_____

_____

_____

_____

Today's Date Is: _____

Things I Did Today: _____

_____

_____

_____

_____

_____

_____

_____

_____

_____

_____

_____

_____

_____

_____

_____

Today's Date Is: _____

Things I Did Today: _____

_____

_____

_____

_____

_____

_____

_____

_____

_____

_____

_____

_____

_____

_____

_____

Today's Date Is: _____

Things I Did Today: _____

_____

_____

_____

_____

_____

_____

_____

_____

_____

_____

_____

_____

_____

Today's Date Is: _____

Things I Did Today: _____

_____
_____
_____
_____
_____
_____
_____
_____
_____
_____
_____
_____
_____
_____
_____

Favorite Toys

Moosie and Goosie are Karen's matching stuffed cats.

How many stuffed animals do you have? _3_

What are their names? _I don't_ _have names for_ _them_

How many dolls do you have? _0_

What are some of your other favorite toys? ___ _play to_

School Stuff

Karen says Ms. Colman is her best teacher ever.

Who is your favorite teacher? _Mrs_
Curtis

What do you like best about him/her? _She_
is   nice

Who is your least favorite teacher? _Mrs_
Smith

What is your best subject? _math_

Worst subject? _reading_

Munchies

Karen loves to eat ice cream and Crunch-O cereal.

What are some of your favorite foods?

pizza _____ no _____

hamburgers _____ yes _____

vegetables _____ no _____

ice cream _____ yes _____

cookies _____ yes _____

yogurt _____ yes _____

other _____ mash patots _____

What are some of your least favorite foods?

_____ carrots _____

Vacations

It's fun to go on vacation!

What was your favorite family vacation? When
we go to florta

What did you see? everything you
would want to see

DISNEY WORLD

CRUISE

How long did it take you to get there? 12 hourz

What was your favorite school trip? to
the zoo

What did you see? _____

Holidays

Karen and Andrew love holidays.

What are your favorite holidays?

Christmas ___ yes ___

Hanukkah ___ no yes ___

Thanksgiving ___ yes ___

Easter ___ yes ___

Passover ___ no yes ___

Halloween ___ yes ___

Fourth of July ___ yes ___

St. Patrick's Day ___ no yes ___

Valentine's Day ___ yes ___

New Year's Day ___ yes ___

other ___ yes ___

Summer Fun

Karen and her friends like to play Going Camping in the summer.

What do you like to do in the summertime?

camp _____ yey _____

swim _____ yey _____

ride my bike _____ yey _____

go to the beach _____ yuy _____

eat ice cream _____ yuy _____

other _____ stay up late _____

All About My Neighborhood

Nancy Dawes lives next door to Karen at the little house. Hannie Papadakis lives across the street and one house down from Karen at the big house.

Who lives next door to you? _____

Who lives across the street? _____

Who lives down the block? _____

_____

Where do your friends live? _____

_____

_____

Nicknames

David Michael calls Karen "Professor" because she wears glasses.

What is your favorite nickname? _Kitty_

_____

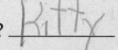

What is your least favorite nickname? _Kristina_

What nicknames do you have for your brothers and/or sisters? _Angie, Sis_

_____

What are your friends' nicknames? _____

_____

Dressing Up

Lovely Ladies is a dress-up game Karen likes to play with her friends. Sometimes Karen wears high heels.

What are some of your favorite dress-up clothes?

_____

_____

_____

What was your best Halloween costume ever?

witch

_____

_____

It's Showtime!

Karen's little brother Andrew likes the TV show *Captain Tornado*.

What are some of your favorite TV shows?

1. _____

2. _____

3. _____

4. _____

Favorite movies?

1. _____

2. _____

3. _____

4. _____

Join the Club!

Once Karen decided to start her own club. She called it the Kittycat Club.

Did you ever have your own club? _____

What was the name of your club? _____

Who was in it? _____
_____

What did you do? _____
_____

How long did your club last? _____

Doodlers' Page

Today's Date Is: _____

Things I Did Today: _____

_____

_____

_____

_____

_____

_____

_____

_____

_____

_____

_____

_____

_____

_____

_____

Today's Date Is: _May 27, 1991_

Things I Did Today: MOM AND DAD
got in a fight
Because of
Uncle Crag

Today's Date Is: _____

Things I Did Today: _____

_____

_____

_____

_____

_____

_____

_____

_____

_____

_____

_____

_____

_____

_____

_____

_____

Today's Date Is: _____

Things I Did Today: _____

_____

_____

_____

_____

_____

_____

_____

_____

_____

_____

_____

_____

_____

_____

_____

_____

Today's Date Is: _____

Things I Did Today: _____

_____

_____

_____

_____

_____

_____

_____

_____

_____

_____

_____

_____

_____

_____

_____

_____

_____

Today's Date Is: _____

Things I Did Today: _____

_____

_____

_____

_____

_____

_____

_____

_____

_____

_____

_____

_____

_____

_____

_____

Today's Date Is: _____

Things I Did Today: _____

_____

_____

_____

_____

_____

_____

_____

_____

_____

_____

_____

_____

_____

_____

_____

Today's Date Is: _____

Things I Did Today: _____

_____

_____

_____

_____

_____

_____

_____

_____

_____

_____

_____

_____

_____

_____

Today's Date Is: _____

Things I Did Today: _____

_____

_____

_____

_____

_____

_____

_____

_____

_____

_____

_____

_____

_____

_____

_____

Today's Date Is: _____

Things I Did Today: _____

_____

_____

_____

_____

_____

_____

_____

_____

_____

_____

_____

_____

_____

_____

_____

Today's Date Is: _____

Things I Did Today: _____

_____

_____

_____

_____

_____

_____

_____

_____

_____

_____

_____

_____

_____

_____

_____

_____

_____

Today's Date Is: _____

Things I Did Today: _____

_____

_____

_____

_____

_____

_____

_____

_____

_____

_____

_____

_____

_____

_____

_____

Today's Date Is: _____

Things I Did Today: _____

_____

_____

_____

_____

_____

_____

_____

_____

_____

_____

_____

_____

_____

_____

_____

Today's Date Is: _____

Things I Did Today: _____

_____

_____

_____

_____

_____

_____

_____

_____

_____

_____

_____

_____

_____

_____

_____

_____

Today's Date Is: _____

Things I Did Today: _____

_____

_____

_____

_____

_____

_____

_____

_____

_____

_____

_____

_____

_____

_____

_____

Today's Date Is: _____

Things I Did Today: _____

_____

_____

_____

_____

_____

_____

_____

_____

_____

_____

_____

_____

_____

_____

_____

Today's Date Is: _____

Things I Did Today: _____

_____

_____

_____

_____

_____

_____

_____

_____

_____

_____

_____

_____

_____

_____

Today's Date Is: _____

Things I Did Today: _____

_____

_____

_____

_____

_____

_____

_____

_____

_____

_____

_____

_____

_____

_____

_____

Today's Date Is: _____

Things I Did Today: _____

_____

_____

_____

_____

_____

_____

_____

_____

_____

_____

_____

_____

_____

_____

_____

_____

Today's Date Is: _____

Things I Did Today: _____

_____

_____

_____

_____

_____

_____

_____

_____

_____

_____

_____

_____

_____

_____

_____

_____

_____

How I Feel

I am happy when _____
_____
_____
_____.

I get mad when _____
_____
_____
_____.

The saddest time I ever had was when _____
_____
_____.

The time I laughed the hardest was when ____
_____
_____
_____.

Eye C U!

Karen wears glasses. She has blue frames for reading and pink frames for the rest of the time.

Do you wear glasses? _____

Who wears glasses in your family? _____

_____

Who wears glasses in your class? _____

_____

What friends wear glasses? _____

_____

Does your teacher wear glasses? _____

Birthdays

For Karen's seventh birthday her dad took her to the Happy-Time Circus.

Which was your favorite birthday? _____
What did you do? _____

Who did you celebrate with? _____
_____

Which was your worst birthday? _____
What was the best birthday party you ever went to? _____
_____

If you were having a birthday party, who would you invite? _____
_____

What would you eat? _____

What games would you play? _____

Rainy Days

Sometimes on rainy days Karen likes to curl up with her special blanket, Tickly, and read a good book.

What do you like to do on rainy days?

read _____

play games _____

watch TV _____

talk on the phone _____

bake cookies _____

draw a picture _____

other _____

_____

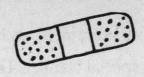

Good Times/Bad Times

What was the best thing that ever happened to
you? _____

_____

_____

What was the worst thing? _____

_____

_____

What was the most embarrassing thing you ever
did? _____

_____

_____

What was the silliest thing you ever did? _____

_____

_____

Haircut Horrors

Once Karen got a horrible haircut at Gloriana's House of Hair. She felt so ugly!

What was your worst haircut? _____

_____

How long did it take for your hair to grow out?

_____

What did your friends say? _____

_____

_____

Color Magic

Karen likes pink. She has two pairs of pink sneakers and a pair of pink glasses.

What is your favorite color? _____
What color do you like the least? _____
_____

Some colors make us feel happy. Other colors make us feel sad. How do you feel when you see the color

blue _____

red _____

yellow _____

black _____

gray _____?

When I Grow Up . . .

What do you want to be when you grow up?

movie star _____

dancer _____

lawyer _____

teacher _____

artist _____

doctor _____

pilot _____

writer _____

other _____

_____

Funny Stuff

On Saturday mornings Karen likes to watch the
TV show *Mister Ed*. Mister Ed is a talking horse.
Karen thinks Mister Ed is very funny.

What TV shows make you laugh?

1. _____

2. _____

3. _____

4. _____

Who is your funniest friend? _____
_____

What is your favorite joke? _____
_____

City Girl/Country Girl

Karen has grandparents who live on a farm in Nebraska.

Do you live in the city or in a town or in the country? _____City_____

What fun things can you do in the country?

_____

_____

_____

What fun things can you do in a big city?

_____

_____

_____

If you could live anywhere in the world, where would you live? _____

_____

_____

Secret Wish

One Christmas, Karen had a very special wish.

If you could have one secret wish, what would it be? _____

_____

_____

_____

_____

_____

_____

Today's Date Is: _____

Things I Did Today: _____

_____

_____

_____

_____

_____

_____

_____

_____

_____

_____

_____

_____

_____

_____

_____

Today's Date Is: _____

Things I Did Today: _____

_____

_____

_____

_____

_____

_____

_____

_____

_____

_____

_____

_____

_____

_____

_____

_____

Today's Date Is: _____

Things I Did Today: _____

_____

_____

_____

_____

_____

_____

_____

_____

_____

_____

_____

_____

_____

_____

_____

_____

_____

Today's Date Is: _____

Things I Did Today: _____

_____

_____

_____

_____

_____

_____

_____

_____

_____

_____

_____

_____

_____

_____

_____

_____

_____

_____

Today's Date Is: _____

Things I Did Today: _____

_____

_____

_____

_____

_____

_____

_____

_____

_____

_____

_____

_____

_____

Today's Date Is: _____

Things I Did Today: _____

_____

_____

_____

_____

_____

_____

_____

_____

_____

_____

_____

_____

_____

_____

_____

Today's Date Is: _____

Things I Did Today: _____

_____

_____

_____

_____

_____

_____

_____

_____

_____

_____

_____

_____

_____

_____

_____

Today's Date Is: _____

Things I Did Today: _____

_____

_____

_____

_____

_____

_____

_____

_____

_____

_____

_____

_____

_____

Today's Date Is: _____

Things I Did Today: _____

_____

_____

_____

_____

_____

_____

_____

_____

_____

_____

_____

_____

_____

_____

_____

Today's Date Is: _____

Things I Did Today: _____

_____

_____

_____

_____

_____

_____

_____

_____

_____

_____

_____

_____

_____

_____

_____

Today's Date Is: _____

Things I Did Today: _____

_____

_____

_____

_____

_____

_____

_____

_____

_____

_____

_____

_____

_____

_____

_____

_____

Today's Date Is: _____

Things I Did Today: _____

_____

_____

_____

_____

_____

_____

_____

_____

_____

_____

_____

_____

_____

_____

_____

_____

Today's Date Is: _____

Things I Did Today: _____

_____

_____

_____

_____

_____

_____

_____

_____

_____

_____

_____

_____

_____

_____

**Look for these
and other books about Karen
in the
Baby-sitters Little Sister series:**